MOUSE
LOVES SPRING

by Lauren Thompson

illustrated by Buket Erdogan

Ready-to-Read

Simon Spotlight

New York   London   Toronto   Sydney   New Delhi

SIMON SPOTLIGHT

An imprint of Simon & Schuster Children's Publishing Division

1230 Avenue of the Americas, New York, New York 10020

This Simon Spotlight edition January 2018

Text copyright © 2005, 2018 by Lauren Thompson

Illustrations copyright © 2005 by Buket Erdogan

Manufactured in the United States of America 1217 LAK

10 9 8 7 6 5 4 3 2 1

ISBN 978-1-5344-0184-6 (pbk)

ISBN 978-1-5344-0185-3 (hc)

ISBN 978-1-5344-0186-0 (eBook)

The illustrations and portions of the text were previously published in 2005 in *Mouse's First Spring*.

One windy spring day,
Mouse and Momma
go out to play.

Mouse sees something **flittery**. What is it?

"A butterfly!"
says Momma.

The wind blows

whoosh!

And the butterfly
flutters away.

Mouse sees something **slimy**. What is it?

"A snail!"
says Momma.

The wind blows

whoosh!

And the snail hides
away.

Mouse sees something **feathery**. What is it?

"A bird!"
says Momma.

The wind blows

whoosh!

And the bird swoops
away.

Mouse sees something
hoppy. What is it?

"A frog!"
says Momma.

The wind blows

whoosh!

And the frog swims away.

Mouse sees something **squiggly**. What is it?

"A worm!"
says Momma.

The wind blows

whoosh!

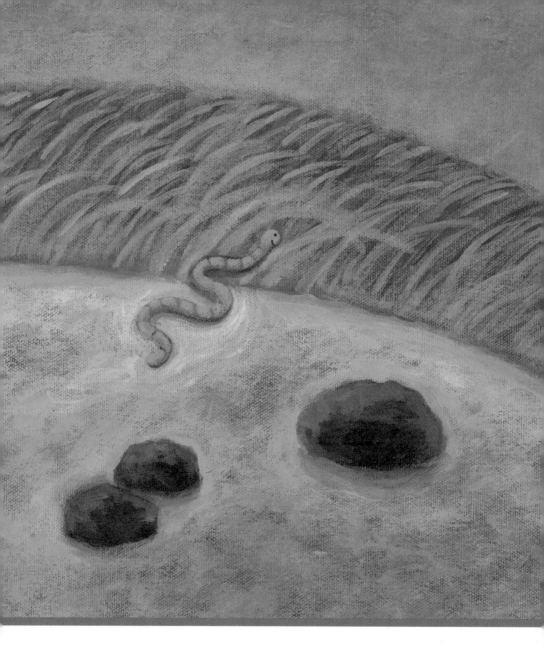

And the worm wiggles
away.

Mouse sees something **petally**. What is it?

"A flower!"
says Momma.

The wind blows

whoosh!

And **Mouse** tumbles
away!

Mouse feels something
warm and **cuddly**.

What is it?

Smooch! A kiss!

Ooch! A hug!

"I love you!"
says Momma.

Mouse and Momma
love spring!

E THOMP   FLT
Thompson, Lauren,
Mouse loves spring /

03/18